D1092568

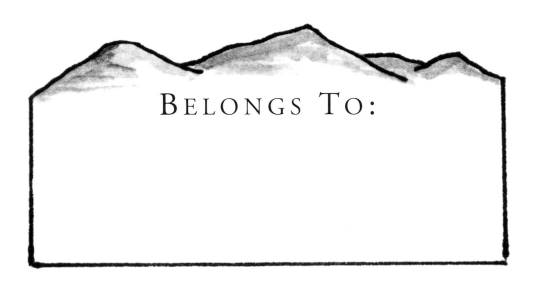

BELONGS TO:

Always Believe in yourself!

Cowgirl Peg

DEDICATION

With love to my parents,
Andy and Johnnie Lea.
They taught me to believe in myself
and I thank them for that.

LIBRARY OF CONGRESS CATALOGING-IN-PUBLICATION DATA
Sundberg, Peggy.
Shortstuff Bucks!
p. cm.
ISBN 0-9721057-4-3 HARDCOVER
1. Horses. 2. Title. 3. Juv. Lit. 4. Cowgirl Peg.
5. Rodeos. 6. Respect. 7. Kindness. 8. Character traits.
2005901660
CIP

Fourth edition printed in Canada by Friesens
Third printing, January 2008

PUBLISHED BY: Cowgirl Peg Enterprises
P.O. Box 56, Wheatland, WY 82201
cowgirlpeg@wildblue.net
www.cowgirlpeg.com

COPYRIGHT: 2005 © Peggy Sundberg
DESIGN BY: F + P Graphic Design, Inc.

Shortstuff Bucks!

Peggy Sundberg

Watercolors by
Pat Wiles

On a bright, sunny day, Shortstuff waited. Today had been a great day for him at the world champion bucking horse rodeo. Now he waited for Cowgirl Peg to take him to his new home — her ranch.

Soon Cowgirl Peg arrived. Rubbing him on the neck, she said "Wow, Shortstuff! I watched you win the championship today. What a grand bucking horse you are!"

"My horses are eager to meet you, so let's get going to your new home." Shortstuff jumped in the trailer and off they went.

Staring at him, Dakota said, "Shortstuff, Cowgirl Peg told us you are the world-champion bucking horse. But we are very curious. You are so SHORT! How did you win?"

"It's a LONG story" said Shortstuff. "Do you want to hear it?"

"YES!" they all answered.

"Well, it all began when I was a baby at Cowboy Jim's ranch. I watched bucking horses in a rodeo and thought it would be fun to jump like that.

So I started running around the pasture, kicking up my heels. The first time I kicked, I fell on my nose. The next time I fell sideways. But I kept trying and soon was able to run and buck at the same time. Next I learned how to jump off of all 4 feet at the same time. That took lots of practice. Soon I added a twist while jumping and bucking.

One afternoon Cowboy Jim watched my practice. He called me to the gate and said 'Shortstuff, you are becoming a really good bucking horse. But you are so SHORT! I just don't think you can ever be in a rodeo unless you grow taller.'

At first I was sad and disappointed. But then I thought 'If I keep practicing, I bet I can be the best bucking horse ever.'

So I didn't give up. Instead, I practiced even more. I ran and jumped. I twisted. I flip-flopped in the air.

Then I asked Cowboy Jim to please let me be a bucking horse in a rodeo. Cowboy Jim looked at me and said, 'Shortstuff, you are just so SHORT! But if you really want to try, I'll take you to the rodeo'.

I was so excited! I could finally try to buck a real cowboy off my back!

That night we went to the rodeo. I was rather nervous, but I knew I could do it.

I got into the bucking chute and the cowboy climbed onto my back. 'This should be an easy ride because you are really SHORT!' he said.

I stood quietly until the gate opened. Then I jumped straight up and burst into the air. The cowboy tried to hold on, but I twisted and flip-flopped. He went flying and landed on his backside in the dirt. 'HA!' I said. 'I might be SHORT, but I know how to buck!'

After that, Cowboy Jim took me to many more rodeos. Cowboys tried and tried to ride me for 8 seconds, but none could. I bucked each one of them into the dirt. Some landed upside-down on their heads, some landed on their noses, others landed on their feet. But no one could ride me.

Then Cowboy Jim decided to enter me in the world champion bucking horse contest. I really had to practice a lot. Each afternoon I ran, jumped, twisted, flip-flopped and bucked as high as I could.

The champion rodeo began a few days ago. The best cowboys in the world would try to ride me for 8 seconds. I wondered if I would be able to buck them off.

Each day a different cowboy tried to ride me. I twisted and turned, flip-flopping while bucking. One-by-one, they landed in the dirt.

Today, the last day
of the contest, the world's best
bucking-horse cowboy tried to
ride me. When he got on my back,
he said 'This should be easy.
You are too SHORT!'

The gate opened and I exploded
into the air. I twisted, I turned, I flip-flopped.
The seconds were counting: 5…6…
I had to get him off my back! So I jumped
straight up, twisted around and
kicked at the same time. The clock struck
7 seconds and the cowboy landed
face-first in the dirt!

I was so excited, I couldn't stop bucking. I bucked all the way around the arena. Then I went back to the cowboy and said 'HA! I might be SHORT, but I know how to buck!'

Throwing his hat into the air, Cowboy Jim hugged me. 'Shortstuff, you might be SHORT, but you are the best bucking horse ever!'

So now I'm visiting Cowgirl Peg's ranch while Cowboy Jim teaches my little brother how to be another great bucking horse."

"We'll enjoy having you as our new friend." said Wise Guy. "But we still want to ask this: You are so SHORT! How did you become the world champion?"

"I might be SHORT" said Shortstuff "but that really was not important. The only thing that mattered was how hard I tried. And I tried really hard!"

Wise Guy and the other horses just looked at Shortstuff and smiled.

Lining up by their new friend as they walked together to the pasture, the horses said, "Shortstuff, what a great story! You might be SHORT, but you are one REALLY COOL HORSE!"

"For all those thousands of kids who have asked the names of all my horses, here they are!"
—Cowgirl Peg

RALPH

DAKOTA

HOLLY

CHANTILLY

SHORTSTUFF

WISE GUY

KATE

ROSIE

BOBBIE

Cowgirl Peg and Wise Guy

ABOUT THE AUTHOR

Peggy Sundberg, now known to thousands of youngsters as "Cowgirl Peg," continually enjoys her new life as an author. She now spends a tremendous amount of time visiting schools nationwide, sharing her books' messages with students of all ages. When at home in the Rocky Mountains she enjoys spending time with her animals, hiking, biking and snowshoeing the slopes, or relaxing at home with loved ones

ABOUT THE ARTIST

Pat Wiles continues to awesomely illustrate the "Cowgirl Peg" books. *Shortstuff Bucks!!* is just another example of her artistic talents. The artwork in this book will amaze adults as well as children. Her wonderful illustrations greatly contribute to the success of these books. When not painting, Pat enjoys ranch life in the mountains with her family and a wide variety of animals, including her rescued wolves.

A COWGIRL PEG BOOK

Other Cowgirl Peg books

Lonesome
the Little Horse
His Mountain Adventure

Based on a true story

Text by
Peggy Sundberg
Watercolor Art by
Pat Wiles

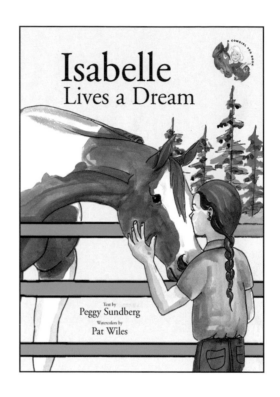

Isabelle
Lives a Dream

Text by
Peggy Sundberg
Watercolors by
Pat Wiles

Jazmine's
Incredible Story

The True Adventures
of Cowgirl Peg's
Beloved Companion

Text by
Peggy
Sundberg
Watercolor Art by
Pat Wiles

Wishful Watoosi
The Horse That Wished He Wasn't

Text by
Corinne Joy Brown
Edited by
Peggy Sundberg
Watercolors by
Pat Wiles

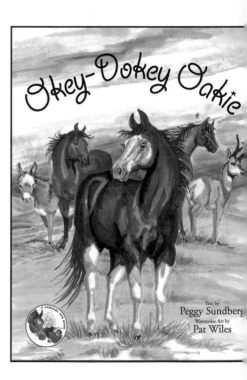

Okey-Dokey Oakie

Text by
Peggy Sundberg
Watercolor Art by
Pat Wiles